15

Snow Day!

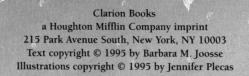

Clarion Books
a Houghton Mifflin Company imprint
215 Park Avenue South, New York, NY 10003
Text copyright © 1995 by Barbara M. Joosse
Illustrations copyright © 1995 by Jennifer Plecas

The illustrations for this book were executed in watercolor, gouache,
colored pencil, and pastel on Strathmore bristol.
The text was set in 15/18-point Berkeley.

Printed in the USA

Library of Congress Cataloging-in-Publication Data

Joosse, Barbara M.
Snow day! / by Barbara M. Joosse ; illustrated by Jennifer Plecas.
p. cm.
Summary: When school is cancelled because of snow, Robby and his
family enjoy the day together.
ISBN 0-395-66588-4
[1. Snow—Fiction. 2. Family life—Fiction.]   I. Plecas, Jennifer, ill.
I. Title.
PZ7.J7435Sn 1995
[E]—dc20   94-17012
CIP
AC
WOZ 10 9 8 7 6 5 4 3 2 1

Snow Day!

By Barbara M. Joosse
Illustrated by Jennifer Plecas

CLARION BOOKS/*New York*

The snow came at night, swirling and swishing.
It piled on the ground in big, whipped peaks.
In the morning, the plow could not get through.
Neither could the school bus.

Robby and Zippy were the first to see the snow.
Robby blew on the windowpane
and watched his breath freeze into lace.
He scratched out his name, R-O-B-B-Y.
Zippy barked at a crow.
His breath froze on the window, too.

"It's a snow day!" Robby yelled,
dancing across the floor in his bare feet,
twirling like the flakes in the sky.
Zippy barked and twirled like a furry flake.

Robby ran to his sister's room.
"There's tons of snow outside!"
he shouted, bouncing on the bed.

Louise looked out the window.
"Wow! I bet they call off school.
Let's go listen to the radio."
   When the radio announcer said their school was closed,
Robby and Louise let out a yelp.
Zippy jumped in the air.
   "I'm going to watch TV," said Louise.
   "It's dumb to waste a snow day on television,"
Robby said to Zippy. "Let's wake up Heather."

"Heather!" Robby said into Heather's sleeping ear.
"It's a snow day. There's no school!"
   "Uh! Good. Wake me for lunch."
Heather was too grown-up to be excited about the snow.
She covered her head with her blanket.
Only her foot stuck out.
Zippy nibbled it.
   "And tell that dog to leave me alone,"
Heather mumbled into her pillow.
   "Mom and Dad get grouchy too when we wake them up,"
Robby whispered to Zippy. "Let's make our own breakfast."

"White bread with powdered sugar would be good
for a snow day," said Robby.
He sifted powdered sugar onto his bread
until it mounded up like snow.
Zippy wanted some, too.
When he barked at the sugar, it flew in the air
and made it look like it was snowing inside.

Mom and Dad came downstairs.

"Oh, my!" said Mom, looking at the sugar-snow.

"It looks like you made your own breakfast."

"Yes," said Robby. "And now we're going outside."

Dad helped Robby button up his jacket.

Robby helped Zippy into his.

Mom put a scarf around Robby's face.

"Have fun, dear," she said.

Robby and Zippy were the first ones to mark up the snow.
They ran and ran, kicking and licking and skidding.
Soon their footprints were everywhere!

Robby pulled his scarf off of his face
and ran up to the living room window.
   "LOUISE!" he shouted.
"LET'S MAKE SNOW ANGELS!"
   Louise looked at Robby's flattened face.
"OK," she said.

Louise and Robby fell onto the snow
and flapped their legs and arms.
    "I'm going to make snow monsters,"
Robby said, squirming in the snow
until it looked like a monster
with two heads.
Zippy made snow dogs.

Dad came out to shovel the driveway.
He lifted off big chunks of snow and piled them to the side.

Zippy and Robby and Louise ran back and forth in Dad's tunnels.
Then they took the chunks of snow and piled them higher.

Dad poked his head above the snow tunnel.
"BOO!" he yelled.
Louise clobbered Dad with snowballs.
He clobbered back.
Pretty soon snowballs were flying everywhere.
Some of them landed on the kitchen door.
"What's going on out here?" asked Mom.

"IT'S A SNOW FIGHT!" everybody yelled.
"Not without me, it isn't."
Mom scooped up a big handful of snow,
squeezed it together, and nailed Dad.
"Whooo-eee!" yelled Dad.
"Men on one side, women on the other."

"That's not fair," shouted Heather,
running outside to join the women's side.
Dad and Robby and Zippy got on one side.
Mom and Louise and Heather got on the other.

Snowballs flew.
Everybody whooped and hollered and threw and ducked
until they fell on the snow, exhausted.
    "Uh-oh, it's snowing again," said Mom.
"It's time for cocoa."

27

Robby and Louise and Heather carried in armloads of wood,
stomping the snow off their boots in the doorway.
Dad piled the wood in the fireplace.
Mom crumpled up a few pieces of paper,
lit a match, and started the fire.

Louise and Heather made cocoa.
Robby put colored marshmallows on top.
He put some in Zippy's dish, too.
Then they sat by the fire, sipping hot chocolate,
and watched the snow fill the windows,
making the whole outside soft and whispery white.

Zippy hogged the blanket.